2.5
177099

D1506087

Papa Gave Me a Stick

By Janice Levy

Illustrated by Simone Shin

STAR BRIGHT BOOKS
CAMBRIDGE, MASSACHUSETTS

Published in the United States of America by Star Bright Books, Inc.
The name Star Bright Books and the Star Bright Books logo are registered
trademarks of Star Bright Books, Inc. Please visit www.starbrightbooks.com.
For bulk orders, please call (617) 354-1300
or email: orders@starbrightbooks.com.

Printed on paper from sustainable forests and a percentage of post-consumer
paper.

Hardback ISBN-13: 978-1-59572-342-0
Paperback ISBN-13: 978-1-59572-343-7

Star Bright Books / MA / 00103150
Printed in China (WKT) 10 9 8 7 6 5 4 3 2 1

Library of Congress Cataloging-in-Publication Data

Levy, Janice.
Papa gave me a stick / by Janice Levy ; illustrated by Simone Shin.
    pages cm
Summary: After seeing a mariachi band, Antonio wants a guitar of his own,
but his father cannot afford one and gives Antonio a stick, instead, which leads
Antonio to perform a series of good deeds, each of which provides a seemingly
useless reward. Includes glossary of Spanish terms.
ISBN 978-1-59572-342-0 (hardcover) – ISBN 978-1-59572-343-7 (pbk.)
[1. Kindness–Fiction. 2. Generosity–Fiction.] I. Shin, Simone, illustrator. II.
Title.
PZ7.L5832Pap 2015
[E]--dc23
                        2014040618

To Rick, with all my love.

A Rick, con todo mi amor. —J.L.

For Thibault—S.S.

"Antonio, listen!" Papa says.
"Here comes the mariachi band!"

Antonio and his father run into the courtyard.

Plink, goes the violin.

Toot, goes the horn.

The mariachis sing as they strum their strings. But Antonio hardly listens. He is too busy staring at the mariachi's guitar.

"I want a *guitarra* . . . one with a felt strap," Antonio says. "Maybe a *guitarra* with a leather strap and fringes. Buy me one, Papa, please?"

Papa frowns. "*Ay, hijo,* I have no money for such things. But I can give you this, my son," he says with a wink and places a stick in Antonio's hand.

Antonio turns away and throws the stick
to the ground. "What good is this?" he says.
He kicks the stick as he walks until he comes
to a shivering dog.

"*¡Qué frío!* I am cold to my bones," howls *el perro.*
"Help me light this fire!"

Antonio pokes his stick under the ashes of the *comal.*
Flames flicker. The grateful dog wags his tail.

"*Gracias, amigo,*" says *el perro.* "This is for you."
He drops a warm tortilla from the oven onto Antonio's lap.
"*¿Una tortilla?*" Antonio says. "What good is this?"

He walks on until he hears a weeping bird.
"*¡Qué hambre!* I am so hungry!" chirps
el pájaro. "I am too weak to build my nest."

Antonio breaks his tortilla into tiny pieces.
The bird gobbles it up and flaps his wings.

"*Gracias, amigo,*" says *el pájaro.* "This is for you."

He drops a string from his beak.

"String?" Antonio says. "What good is this?"

Antonio walks on until a donkey blocks his path.

"*¡Qué dolor!* Ouch! What a toothache!" brays *el burro.* "Help me yank out my rotten tooth!"

Antonio ties his string around the donkey's tooth and pulls. Out it pops. The donkey clicks his heels.

"Gracias, amigo," says *el burro.* "This is for you."

He shakes a blanket off his back.

"A blanket?" Antonio says. "What good is this?"

He walks on until he comes to a cat splashing in a stream.

"*¡Qué miedo!* I'm so afraid!" meows *el gato*. "I chased this fat rat and gulp, I—can't—swim!"

Antonio throws one end of his blanket into the water and pulls the cat to shore.

"*Gracias, amigo,*" says *el gato*. "This is for you."

He slips a gold ring off his collar.

"A gold ring?" Antonio says. "What good is this?"

Antonio walks on until he comes to a church.
A bride stands alone at the altar, scowling and
tapping her foot. The mariachi band plays louder.
The groom crawls on his knees among the pews.

"*¡Qué pena!* I am such a fool," says *el novio.*
"I have lost the wedding ring. What can I do?"

Antonio hands the groom his gold ring and
points to the bride.

"*Gracias, amigo,*" says *el novio*. "This is for you."
He takes his guitar and places the strap over
Antonio's shoulder.

"*¡Una guitarra!*" Antonio says, running all the way home. "Now this is good for me!"

"Papa, look!" he says. "I gave my stick to *el perro* . . .

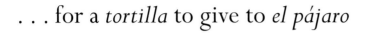
. . . for a *tortilla* to give to *el pájaro*

. . . for a string to give to *el burro*

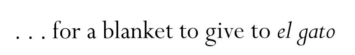

. . . for a blanket to give to *el gato*

. . . for a ring to give to *el novio*

. . . for *una guitarra!*"

"*¡Qué bueno!* Good for you!" Papa laughs.
"All that to earn your *guitarra*."

"By the way, Papa," Antonio asks.
"Did you ever have a *guitarra*?"

"I did when I was little," Papa says. "A beautiful one with a leather strap and fringes. Just like the mariachi."

"How did you get your *guitarra*?" Antonio asks.

Papa shrugs. "My papa gave me a stick. . . ."

GLOSSARY

hijo (EEE-ho): son

¡Qué frío! (keh FREE-oh): How cold!

el perro (el PEH-rro): the dog

comal (co-MAHL): oven

gracias (GRA-cee-ahs): thank you

amigo (ah-MEE-go): friend

¡Qué hambre! (keh HAHM-breh): What hunger!

el pájaro (el PA-ha-ro): the bird

¡Qué dolor! (keh doh-LOR): What pain!

el burro (el BUH-rro): the donkey

¡Qué miedo! (keh mee-EH-doh): What fear!

el gato (el GA-toh): the cat

¡Qué pena! (keh PEH-na): How embarrassing!

el novio (el NO-vee-o): the groom

¡Qué bueno! (keh boo-EH-no): Great!

MARIACHI BAND INSTRUMENTS

Violín/Violin

Guitarrón

Vihuela

Trompeta/Trumpet

Guitarra/Guitar